FARMER JOE'S FAINTING GOATS to the RESCUE!

Brenda Ruppert Bunkers

Illustrations by Blueberry Illustrations

Disclaimer

Copyright © 2021
All Rights Reserved.

No part of this book can be transmitted or reproduced in any form,
including print, electronic, photocopying, scanning, mechanical,
or recording, without prior written permission from the author.

This book has been written for entertainment purposes only. Every effort has been
made to make this book as complete and accurate as possible. However, there
may be mistakes in typography or content. Also, this book provides information
only up to the publishing date, so it may not include some information.

The purpose of this book is to entertain children and teach them the values of
companionship, helping out, and kindness. The author and the publisher do not
warrant that the information contained in this book is fully complete and shall not
be responsible for any errors or omissions. The author and publisher shall have
neither liability nor responsibility to any person or entity with respect to any loss
or damage caused or alleged to be caused directly or indirectly by this book.

ISBN: 978-0-578-93134-0

I would like to dedicate this book to my nine grandchildren—
Avery, Easton, Abe, Jaden, Dawson, Landon, Miles, Jayce, and Maverick. It
was your personalities that inspired me to write this story. I adore your smiles,
cherish your hugs, and admire your hearts, and I will love you all forever!

I would also like to thank my children, Justin (Krissa), Nic (Lisa), and
Stephanie (JJ), who have blessed me with these nine grandchildren.

Grandpa Dale Bunkers, you are the fatherly figure I chose to
use for Farmer Joe. I would like to thank you for being a
part of our lives and guiding us with the utmost integrity.

And most importantly, I would like to thank my husband, Dean. You have
been a joy to share my life with for 40 years now, and I will love you forever!

Contents

Chapter 1: Life at Farmer Joe's Farm … 5

Chapter 2: The Fainting Goats … 10

Chapter 3: Avery … 14

Chapter 4: Easton … 22

Chapter 5: Abe … 29

Chapter 6: Jaden … 35

Chapter 7: Dawson … 39

Chapter 8: Landon … 46

Chapter 9: Miles … 53

Chapter 10: Jayce … 58

Chapter 11: Success of Working Together … 66

Chapter 12: Welcome Back, Farmer Joe! … 70

Chapter 13: An Unexpected Guest … 75

Chapter 14: The Soccer Match … 84

Chapter 1: Life at Farmer Joe's Farm

Farmer Joe woke up to a sunny day outside, with just a hint of chill in the air to remind him that winter was nearing its end. He could feel pain in his ankles and back, but he ignored it as he sat up in his bed. The sunlight streaming in through the sheer curtains of his room was warm and inviting, and Farmer Joe could not help but feel his spirits rise as he threw the curtains aside and gazed out onto the green pastures and the neighboring farms around. The trees were swaying in the slight wind, and he could see some of his neighbors and friends already out and about, bustling with their morning routine, fussing about their little children, feeding their animals, and working on their farms.

A little distance away from the entire hustle and bustle, Farmer Joe spied his small herd of goats munching on grass and hopping here and there. He squinted his eyes to get a clearer view. Though his eyesight had weakened over the years, he could still manage to see enough without his eyeglasses. The goats had been with him for as long as he could remember and were the only family he had. He still remembered the first time he laid eyes on them, and instead of returning home with just four, he brought all eight home as he could not bear to separate them. He adored his goats, and they loved him back.

From a distance, it almost looked like the goats were talking and playing with each other. It was a heartening sight to see. Farmer Joe chuckled to himself. This is exactly what they looked like when Farmer Joe had gone to the town market that fateful day and saw them playing in the pen. The goats were smaller back then, but every bit as cute and playful as they are now. Farmer Joe let out a hearty laugh after he witnessed a 10-minute show of the owner

Jules
Abe
Avery
Miller
Declan
Landon
Easton
Jayce

chasing one of the goats, and as soon as he got close, it fainted. The goats would dramatically roll over on the grass with their hooves pointed toward the sun and play dead for a moment. Immediately, Farmer Joe knew he wanted all of them. He emptied out his pockets and handed the owner all the money he carried with him that day. The goats were then loaded onto a truck. Now, that sounds easier said than done because if you have ever been around fainting goats, you would know why they have such a strange name—fainting goats faint when strangers approach them. Loading the goats onto a pickup truck took an hour because the goats would keep fainting as soon as Farmer Joe or the owner tried to pick them up. Instead of being annoyed, Farmer Joe was amused. Some of them had to be physically carried off the truck and into the barn when they arrived home. Ever since then, the goats had become the life and joy of Farmer Joe's farm.

Farmer Joe's stomach growled loudly, reminding him that he had been staring out the window for the past 15 minutes.

He giggled slightly and thought, "Better get me some breakfast."

He slipped into his fuzzy slippers and waddled his way to the kitchen, put on some coffee to brew, and made a plate of scrambled eggs and sausage. He then toasted two slices of bread and poured his cup of coffee. He set the kitchen table and looked on with satisfaction at the quick but hearty breakfast he had managed to make for himself.

The kitchen window had a clear view of his barn, and looking at the sad, forsaken structure, it reminded him of what he had been ignoring for months. The doors were splintering in places and were in desperate need of paint, including water pipes that needed repair. The ditches around the farm were overgrown with weeds, shrubs needed to be trimmed, and the red fence, that was once most breathtaking, was falling apart.

For the past few months, Farmer Joe had not really focused much on anything besides caring for his goats. He had not been feeling well for a while now; he got tired quickly and ran out of breath. His joints had started aching, and even rounding up his naughty goats got a bit too much sometimes. He had been thinking of visiting the doctor in the nearby town, but he kept putting it off.

The farm had always been his home. He had grown up here, and there were countless childhood memories attached to the barn. As a young boy, Farmer Joe loved playing in the hay loft, building tunnels and secret passageways. He remembered his grandpa and father teaching him how to do basic repair work around the farm when he got a bit older. He eagerly helped his parents out at the farm and had a bunch of friends from nearby farms that he was still friends with. In early spring, finding a new litter of baby kittens was always a delight.

Farmer Joe was proud and fond of his farm. It was handed down to him from his parents and their parents before that. The barn was hand-built by his grandfather in earlier years, and Farmer Joe had made some changes and kept the farm in great condition as long as he could. But for the past few months, he had not really felt up to it.

He looked over at the dry, overgrown, and uncared-for piece of land where he used to grow all sorts of vegetables and herbs. Potatoes, tomatoes, corn, lettuce, turnips, radishes, and many others! Farmer Joe had not grown anything there for a while, especially since winter arrived. Now that spring was here, many of his neighbors were busy preparing their lands for planting crops. He knew he had to do the same and repair his barn and fences immediately.

He went into the basement to look for his toolbox and other instruments he would need for repairs. When he walked out of the house, he could feel his spirit sinking already. The barn looked terrible and far worse than he had expected. The repairs would take weeks or even months! He was not young anymore, and he knew he could not work at the same pace and with the same energy that he used to. His friends used to assist him with small repairs around the farm before, but now he was on his own. Sighing, Farmer Joe got to work. He had delayed it long enough.

Chapter 2: The Fainting Goats

Anyone passing by the farm could hear Farmer Joe grunting and groaning inside from fixing the leaking pipe in his barn. A few minutes of kneeling on the ground reminded Farmer Joe of his age. His joints were aching, and he needed frequent breaks to catch his breath and relax his cramping muscles. Frustrated, he threw his pliers on the ground and sat down with his back rested against the barn's wall, panting with his head in his hands.

He did not realize how long he sat there, but he looked up to see all eight of his goats—Avery, Easton, Abe, Jaden, Dawson, Landon, Miles, and Jayce—peeking around from the door of the barn, looking at Farmer Joe with curiosity. They almost looked concerned, and Farmer Joe could not help but smile.

"Shoo, everything is okay. Go play."

The goats scattered after a while as Farmer Joe got to his feet.

"I guess today is as good as any day to visit the doctor," he mumbled to himself. "I might as well pick up supplies and paint for all the repairs needed." He went inside his farmhouse, got his wallet and the keys to his truck, and rode off on the dirt road toward the doctor's office.

His doctor was a kind young man who had been tending to him for the past year or so.

"Farmer Joe! I am so happy to see you!" he exclaimed in delight as he saw Farmer Joe entering the clinic.

Avery
Easton
Dawson
Miles
Jayce
Linson
Jaden
Abe
11

Farmer Joe told him about the pain in his joints and how tired he gets even when doing light work. He saw Dr. Allen grow more and more worried as he talked and answered his questions.

"You shouldn't have waited so long before coming to see me, Farmer Joe," he told him in a slightly concerned tone. "I'm writing down some tests that I need you to get done from the hospital, then come back and we will talk again."

"Yes, Sir." Farmer Joe took the piece of paper from the doctor's hand and tried to read what it said but did not understand a single word.

"Don't worry, the staff at the hospital will know what to do."

Farmer Joe made his way to the ground floor, where the tests were to be conducted. The next 2 or 3 hours went by as Farmer Joe was directed from one room to the next and underwent several tests. One nurse stuck a needle in his arm and drew blood, and another asked him to lay still while they took x-rays of his body.

After a few minutes of waiting, Dr. Allen approached him and gently put a hand on his shoulder. "I think it would be a good idea if you stay over at the hospital for a few days until the test results are in. I want to keep an eye on you," he said kindly.

"Is everything okay, doctor?"

"I hope so. But meanwhile, I really think a hospital stay would do you good." He could see Farmer Joe was not too excited about the idea.

All Farmer Joe could think about was his goats. He had never really been sick or been away from the farm. What would his goats do without him? Who would feed them?

After a minute of thinking about it, he said, "Okay, I'll just run uptown to gather my supplies for the repairs needed on the farm and then head home to gather a few items and speak to my neighbor about caring for my goats."

Farmer Joe reached home and told his old friend and neighbor, Matt, about the situation and asked him to take care of his goats until he returned from the hospital. Matt assured him that his goats were in good hands and that he should not be worrying about anything at all.

At last, he went to his fainting goats to feed them one last time before leaving for the hospital. They saw him coming and ran over to him, the youngest of them tripping while hurrying to get to Farmer Joe.

As he fed them, he talked to them as he always did. Farmer Joe explained the delayed farm repairs, his ailing health, and what the doctor had said. He petted all of them one by one as he bid farewell. He knew it was only going to be a short hospital stay, but he was going to miss his little darlings.

Chapter 3: Avery

Avery watched Farmer Joe's truck disappear down the road. She was worried for Farmer Joe. He did not specify how long he would be gone, but he seemed really sad when saying goodbye. Avery had been observing how Farmer Joe was getting old and having trouble doing much around the farm.

She could hear her brothers laughing and squealing behind her. She turned around and saw that they had already dispersed and were running and laughing around.

"Tag," Landon ran by, tagging her to play with them, but Avery was not in the mood.

They were probably too young to understand how sick Farmer Joe was getting and how his health had deteriorated over the past year.

She rolled her eyes at her brothers. Jayce and Miles were giggling on the grass, and the rest of them were talking and munching.

Avery really wanted to help Farmer Joe, but she did not know how. He had done so much for them over the years. She was the oldest of the goats, and being the only girl in the pack, had shared a much closer bond with Farmer Joe than her younger brothers. While they were off goofing around and playing in the fields, Avery would sometimes stick by Farmer Joe as he worked on the farm and would try to keep him company or help in any way. She felt miserable thinking that she could not help him out when he needed it the most.

Jayce
Miles
Dawson
Avery
Landon
Easton
Abe
Jaden
15

As she was gazing off into the distance thinking, she saw Jayce exiting the farm through the gap in the fence. Avery remembered that the barn used to be in perfect condition when the goats had first arrived there. But in the past year, it had started to fall apart. Farmer Joe had been trying to mend things at the farm, but now that he had fallen ill, Avery was not sure whether he would be able to continue.

"I know!" she exclaimed suddenly to nobody. "I know what we can do for Farmer Joe."

She started getting really excited as the plan quickly formed in her head. We could repair the farm for Farmer Joe in his absence and surprise him when he comes back!

"Oh, how happy he would be to see his barn looking as good as new!" she squealed in delight. She could not wait to share the idea with her brothers. She was sure they will be as excited about it as she was. They all adored Farmer Joe from the depths of their hearts and would love to do something nice for him.

In a few minutes, she had managed to gather all her siblings in the middle of the field. While Jayce and Miles came grumbling because Avery had interrupted their playtime, they had to listen as Avery was their older sister.

"What do you want to talk to us about?" Abe inquired curiously.

She could see Jayce squirming, eager to get done with it and return to playing. Miles kicked him in the hoof, but both made a straight face when they saw Avery looking at them sternly.

"I have a great idea. I was thinking of doing something special for Farmer Joe when he gets back from the hospital, but I need help from all of you."

"What do you have in mind?" asked Jaden with his interest piqued.

"Okay, so we all know the farm is very dear to Farmer Joe, right? It is not in the best condition right now, and Farmer Joe had wanted to make some repairs." She gestured around the farm, and the other goats also swept their eyes over the mess the farm had become.

"I was thinking … how about we repair the farm in Farmer Joe's absence? We could patch up the fence and paint it, trim the shrubs, and make the barn look as good as new. I'm sure Farmer Joe would be delighted to see that!"

All her brothers were looking at her with their eyes sparkling with excitement, except Landon.

"Does that mean we have to work?" he grumbled.

But the others were extremely excited.

"Yes, let's do it!" exclaimed Abe.

"That's a great idea!" said Easton and Dawson.

"Ooh, I'm so excited already!" piped in Jayce as he started jumping up and down in joy.

"Hush, calm down, Jayce!" said Avery laughing.

"So, tell us what we have to do," said Miles.

All of them were looking at Avery expectantly. They all looked up to her because she had always been the wise and responsible older sibling. She realized that if she wanted to get this done by the time Farmer Joe got back, she would have to supervise the entire thing. Leaving her brothers on their own would result in a disaster. She could count on Abe, Easton, and Jaden to help her plan this, but the younger siblings must be told what to do.

"Uh, okay, I will draw up a list of things that need to be done and then divide the tasks among us all. Sound good?"

"Yes!" came the synchronized response.

Avery got right down to business. She went around the farm and made a mental note of everything that the goats can fix. She then went to the basement where she knew Farmer Joe kept his tools and supplies.

They were in luck. Farmer Joe had gone shopping for the supplies before he came home that day. There were cans of paint, paintbrushes, pliers, hammers, nails, and hand pruners.

"Perfect!" she smiled to herself. "We have everything we need."

The supplies looked heavy, so she went back upstairs to ask some of her older brothers to help her carry the stuff to the barn. She wanted them to start working immediately. She had overheard Farmer Matt saying that Farmer Joe might be coming home from the hospital in two to three days. Avery knew they would need to work hard and fast if they want to surprise Farmer Joe.

She called Abe, Easton, and Jaden and asked them to help in hauling the supplies upstairs. She saw the three of them joking and pushing each other up the stairs. As soon as Abe reached the landing, he turned around and locked the basement door, trapping Jaden and Easton inside. As the two of them banged on the basement door, Abe cracked up with laughter.

Avery rolled her eyes and opened the lock. Easton and Jaden burst through the door and ran after Abe, who ran as fast as he could to get away. They had forgotten all their supplies in the process.

"Stop it, guys. There is no time to play around," Avery called out. She could not understand why her brothers could not take anything seriously enough.

Her three brothers made a face, and she heard them whisper "party pooper" behind her.

Avery was always focused on her work. She believed that there is a time for work and play and that these two should not be mixed. Her brothers adored and admired her always. Her dedication, practicality, and straightforwardness would take her far.

The seven brothers stood around the pile of supplies and waited for Avery to give out the instructions.

"Abe and Easton, you are in charge of mending the fences all around the farm."

Both the boys nodded in acknowledgment and high-fived each other. Easton picked up the wooden planks, while Abe got the nails and hammer.

"Jaden, pick up the pack of seeds for all the vegetables and herbs and do whatever is needed to make the field ready for planting."

Jaden picked up the heavy burlap bag filled with seeds, a shovel, and a hand pruner.

"Dawson, you are in charge of cleaning out the barn and making it neat and organized."

"Yes, ma'am!" said Dawson as he picked up the broom and rake.

She saw Landon snickering and knew what task to assign him.

"Landon, you will be fixing the leaking water pipe in the barn and helping Dawson out if he needs it."

"What? No! Can't I have something fun to do?"

"No." Avery gave a blunt reply and moved onto the next goats.

"Miles, you will be painting the fences after Abe and Easton are done repairing them."

"Oh, yeah!" said an excited Miles as he picked up one heavy bucket of paint.

"Jayce, you're with me. We'll be painting the barn's exterior." Avery kept this for herself because she loved drawing and painting. She already had many ideas about how she wanted to paint the barn.

"Nooooo!" whined Jayce, "I wanna be with Miles!"

"But you're not. You are with me, and we will have lots of fun."

Jayce started to complain, but Avery cut him off with a look.

"So, if everybody has taken what they need, you can all get to work now. Let's meet again in the field at 5 o'clock."

Chapter 4: Easton

As Easton and Abe walked over to the broken fence, Easton looked around and took in the condition of the fence wall. Once red and beautiful, the fence was now dulled, chipped, and missing sections in so many places. It had been exposed to harsh sunlight during the summers and chilly rains in the winters. It was a sad picture to look at. The fence circling the farm was one of the most distinctive features of Farmer Joe's farm. Anybody approaching from a distance could spot the red fences and recognize the barn.

Abe had by now picked up a broken plank and was pretending to swordfight with it. He came at Easton and poked him lightly in the stomach with it. Abe was always the monkey of the group, constantly cracking jokes in the most awkward and unsuitable situations.

"Easton, what do you call a cow mowing the lawn?" called out Abe. "A lawn mooooer!" he said laughing.

Avery often considered Easton to be her second-in-command and relied on him to communicate things in a more friendly way. He was the tallest brother of the group, even if he and Abe were the same age.

Right now, Abe was balancing several fence planks on his horns and showing off how strong he was. He could get a little too confident at times. He picked up another plank to put on the pile, and the whole thing came crashing down, making him collapse to the ground.

Easton shook his head and despite himself laughed at how comical Abe looked. Sheepishly, Abe stood up and brushed himself off.

Abe
Easton

"Okay, so let's get down to work, shall we?" called Easton, realizing they have already wasted precious time standing there.

"Abe, you start from that corner," directed Easton, pointing to the far north side. "And I'll start here. We'll meet in the middle when we are done."

"Yes, sir," mumbled Abe. He lifted his planks and other tools and was off on his way.

Easton set to work too.

The morning was pleasant—not too hot, not too cold. And while the two goats worked on the fences, time seemed to pass by pleasantly enough.

A little while later, Easton heard small hoof steps behind him and turned around to see Miles trotting up to him with a bucket of red paint.

"What are you doing here, Miles?" Easton called out.

"Avery asked me to paint the fences, so here I am," chirped Miles.

Easton eyed him for a minute. "Yeah, but why are you so late then?"

A flash of guilt crossed Miles' face. "Um, well, I kinda went to chase Farmer Matt's sheep for a while."

"Typical Miles," thought Easton to himself. He was always doing mischievous things.

"Okay, fine, you can start painting from there," said Easton, and he walked him over to where the fence was repaired already. Easton showed Miles how to paint and use the brush to make long strokes over the fence. He stood over and saw Miles practicing his strokes, and when he was sure that he had gotten the hang of it, Easton went back to his work.

He looked over at Abe and saw him running laps with the neighbor's horse.

Shaking his head, he just decided to get back to his own work. He pulled out the broken fences, put in new wooden planks, and all the while kept whistling to himself, getting lost in his work.

After a while, he spied Miles sleeping on the grass in the distance, his paint can next to him. Abe and Easton had finished repairing a considerable part of the fence wall, and Miles had not even covered a quarter of it in the past few hours. At this rate, who knows how long he will take to finish the entire fence. Easton was somewhat amused and annoyed. He was going to go up to Miles and shake him awake. But then he saw Abe walking toward him too. He had the most mischievous grin on his face, and Easton immediately understood what he was going to do. He could not help but let an identical grin creep across his face as well.

Both the brothers tiptoed up to Miles while he was fast asleep. Easton picked up the paint can, while Abe picked up the brush, and together they painted Miles' small horns red and put red circles on his nose and cheeks. He looked comical, as the red stood out starkly against his otherwise spotless white fur.

Easton and Abe exchanged a look, and despite trying to control it, burst out laughing.

Miles jumped up, startled by the noise, and then relaxed when he saw Easton and Abe. Easton knew that Miles really liked him. Easton was just cool that way. All his brothers adored him, and while they were a little intimidated sometimes by Avery's strong personality, Easton's easygoing but responsible nature made them all very comfortable.

"Oh, geez! Sorry, Easton, I think I dozed off for a while."

He looked so adorable standing there looking at Easton with his big brown eyes and his red face and horns. All Easton could manage was a nod as he and Abe held back another bout of laughter.

With a serious expression, Easton told Miles, "Listen, it is okay, but you know we must get done with this by the time Farmer Joe is back, right? Don't you want to give him a happy Welcome Home, Miles?"

"I do! I really, really do. I miss him already," the little goat exclaimed.

"Well then, we have to stop slacking off and get really serious about our work here, or we won't get done in time, and it will ruin our surprise. Do you understand?"

Miles was looking up at him with round, sincere eyes, and he nodded his head with enthusiasm.

"Off you go then. Back to work," said Easton.

Miles darted away and obediently picked up his can and started painting. He can be naughty and distracted, but he listens to his older siblings.

As soon as Miles walked away, Easton and Abe collapsed on the ground, laughing till their stomachs hurt. They could not wait for the other goats to notice little Miles' face and horns.

As Easton worked, the other animals from neighboring farms said "Hi" to him whenever they walked past the other side of the fence. Easton made small conversation with some of them but kept working alongside. Easton had a lot of friends in the area. Almost everybody from the surrounding farms was on good terms with him. It had always been like that. Easton never had any trouble making friends. It just came naturally to him; he never had to try too hard. A lot of them also came to him for advice, because he was known for being sensible and never showing favoritism.

Just then, a cow from Farmer Matt's farm walked up to Easton and greeted him. Easton welcomed her with a big grin too. She seemed troubled, but before Easton could ask her what was wrong, she launched into her story.

"So, I need to talk to you about something. This cow at the barn is acting very nasty with me, and I think she has turned all the other cows against me too. I do not understand what happened. She was my best friend and I'm confused about what I should do now."

Easton listened carefully and thought for a minute.

"You could ask her directly, you know. You might have unintentionally hurt her or something, which is why she is acting this way. In any case, it is best to talk it out with her."

"Yeah, okay." She seemed distracted. "Thanks for the advice, Easton. I know I can always count on you."

"Do you need some help with that?" she asked, eyeing the fence.

Easton said, "You'll probably end up hammering your hoof."

"Ha." She rolled her eyes and walked slowly back to her barn, while Easton finished his side of the fence.

Chapter 5: Abe

Abe found the work interesting enough for himself. It was quite some time into his work, but he wasn't even feeling tired. Abe could power through anything when he wanted to. He was used to running around and playing all day, and it took a lot for Abe to get tired. He was more into sports than any of his other siblings. Even when he was little, he used to chase children's soccer balls around the field. The passion never died down, and as he got older, he developed a keen interest in soccer. The neighborhood goats and even his siblings would sometimes join in on the matches, and the whole field would be scattered with a bunch of goats playing soccer. Abe was the best of them, of course. Nobody could compete with him.

Part of the reason he was so good at the game was because he always made it a point to practice hard. No matter how busy he was, whether he had someone to play with, Abe would pick up a ball every day and toss it around for a while, practicing his kicks. He was very dedicated and organized when it came to sports and took it very seriously.

A few months ago, Abe had been invited to a regional soccer game in a neighboring town just 10 miles away from their own farm. His friend Sydney from Farmer Matt's farm had shown him the poster and invitation where it was stated that the winner would receive a cash prize of $500 and all the players would get a signed soccer ball from a legendary soccer player.

When Abe heard that, he was unable to control his excitement and immediately ran to Farmer Joe for permission to sign up for the game. That day Farmer Joe

Miles
Landon
Dawson
Abe

was busy making apple jam. Avery and Dawson were helping Farmer Joe cut and peel the apples. Abe rushed past them and went right up to Farmer Joe. In a hurried manner, he told him about the selection for the regional soccer game and all the gifts and cash that would be awarded to the winning team. Farmer Joe asked Abe to slow down as he was unable to comprehend what Abe was trying to say. So, Abe started all over again.

But Farmer Joe was still terribly busy stirring the apple jam and checking its consistency. In his desperation, Abe yanked Farmer Joe's sleeve. The wooden ladle spoon fell right out of Farmer Joe's hand and hit Abe on the head. Abe's head and face were covered with red, sticky apple jam.

Avery and Dawson had tried to contain their laughter. They exchanged glances and both knew that Abe deserved it. It was wrong of him to disturb Farmer Joe like that. But when they saw Farmer Joe wiping the jam away from Abe's head and face, they rushed to help. Avery told Dawson to wipe the apple jam that had fallen on the floor. She took Abe to the kitchen sink and helped him wash his head and face. The gooey apple jam was stuck on his brown fur and it took a while for it all to be washed clean.

Avery told Abe to be patient and discuss the matter with Farmer Joe over dinner. She told him to apologize to Farmer Joe for yanking his sleeve and making a mess in the kitchen. Abe agreed and stayed over to help Avery, Dawson, and Farmer Joe store the apple jam in small Mason jars.

At the dinner table, Farmer Joe asked Abe about the regional soccer match. Abe gave him all the information that Sydney had given to Abe. He showed the poster and the invitation letter to Farmer Joe. On the back of the invitation letter there was a form that had to be completed.

Abe needed Farmer Joe's permission and signature to sign up for the soccer match. Farmer Joe told Abe that he did not mind taking him to the soccer match, but it was only possible if Farmer Matt was available that day to drive his truck. Farmer Joe's pickup truck had become old and rusty. It was not safe to travel 10 miles in an old and rusty pickup truck with young goats.

"I can talk to Sydney and he can ask Farmer Matt if he is free that day," said Abe.

"Sure. But remember to take the apple jams with you and don't insist if he says he will be busy that day."

Farmer Joe knew that Abe's main motivation for attending the tryouts was the cash prize and soccer ball signed by a legendary soccer player.

The next day, Farmer Matt agreed to take Abe, Sydney, and Farmer Joe to the tryouts. Avery was asked to be in charge for the day. She promised Farmer Joe that she will look after her younger brothers until they returned.

Farmer Joe, Farmer Matt, Abe, and Sydney left the farm early in the morning. They had reached the soccer field by 10:30 a.m. Abe and Sydney looked at all the older goats in awe. They were so tall and muscular and could kick the soccer ball with such force. Farmer Joe led the way and they reached the table where the selection committee was seated. One of the three men looked at Farmer Joe and asked who will be signing up for the selection match.

Farmer Joe pointed at Abe and handed the form over to the man in a blue jacket. All three men eyed Abe. They looked at each other and exclaimed, "But he is too young!"

"We are looking for older goats."

Abe pleaded, "But I play well. I have been practicing for years. I score all the goals when my brothers and I play together."

"Abe, we are sure you are a great player, but you are not old enough. Tell you what … come here again in a couple of years and then we will let you play against older goats because right now, even if we select you, your team could get disqualified in the regionals for having a younger goat on their team. Now you wouldn't want that, would you?" Abe shook his head. He was disappointed but understood what the man meant. He was deeply sorry about troubling Farmer Joe and Farmer Matt. As they turned around to leave the playing field, the third man called out, "If you want, you can stay and watch the other goats play. You might learn a few things from them."

Abe's face lit up. He had a broad smile. He looked at Farmer Joe and Farmer Matt for approval. Both nodded their heads in agreement. Sydney was equally delighted. The four of them took their places at the spectators stand and watched the older goats play.

Since that day, Abe had been practicing the kicks and other techniques that he had learned from the older goats. He was now excited about trying for the next regional game as soon as he was old enough and for that, he was willing to practice hard every day.

So even in between mending the fences, Abe decided to sneak off for a quick match with his friends while Easton was teaching Miles how to paint.

He spied two of his friends walking off in the distance, and he quickly got a soccer ball and kicked it with all his might toward them. It hit one of them on the head, and they came running over. They flung the ball back at Abe, but Abe was quick and he easily dodged it, giggling. The three of them were soon involved in a heated match, where the other two were competing against Abe, but Abe was clearly winning. They played for a while. The boys then randomly fooled around. They sprinted against each other and tackled each other to the ground. When Abe got back, with messy hair and a scratched knee, he had more energy than before and quickly picked up from where he left off.

While Abe took a lot of breaks and spent some time racing around the field with his friends, he was done with his part of the fence before Easton. He was always fast when he wanted to be. He always timed himself well and got done with his work no matter how much time he spent wasting away.

Chapter 6: Jaden

Jaden started walking in the opposite direction as the others, because the field was located on the backside of the barn. He knew he was in for a quiet day, but he did not mind. Jaden always took his work seriously, and he did not really appreciate distractions and disturbances. When he worked, he put all his mind and heart into what he was doing. Had one of the younger goats been sent to help him, he knew he would not have gotten any work done at all. He whistled as he made his way around the barn. As he emerged from the side and had his first glimpse of the field, he stopped and let out a long whistle.

"That seems like a lot of work," he said out loud to himself.

The field was overgrown with shrubs, and it was so thick with growth that he could not see the ground anymore. Dry bushes dotted the field, and the soil seemed dry. Farmer Joe had even stocked the old wheelbarrow with tools.

Jaden knew that it would be bad, but he did not expect it to be this bad.

Although it seemed daunting, Jaden loved a good challenge. He set down the supplies at the edge of the field and went about picking up the random trash that had collected there. After he had disposed of it in a plastic bag, he picked up his hand pruner. The first day was probably going to be spent removing the shrubs and overgrowth.

Sighing, Jaden went into the field and started chopping away. He hurt his hoof a bit as he stepped on a sharp twig. He sat down to nurse it, and as soon as the stinging feeling faded, he got back to work. Things needed to be ready in time for Farmer Joe's arrival, and it would never happen if he sat down to nurse every little cut and scratch.

SEED
SEED
SEED
SEED
Jaden
36

Minutes turned into hours as Jaden worked hard to make the field look presentable. He took little breaks in between when his hooves started aching from working the hand pruner. He had a big water bottle with him that he drank from whenever he got thirsty. The sun was starting to fall from the sky, and he figured it must be around 3 o'clock.

"I should ask Abe to have soccer practice this evening when we are done with work," thought Jaden.

Jaden loved sports too, much like Abe. Abe taught him to play, and even though he is a little younger, he had picked up on the game fast. Last evening, Abe told Jaden that he was proud of him, and Jaden felt happy to hear that.

With renewed vigor, Jaden started working again, excited about the evening match with Abe. As he worked, he started humming the tune to a chorus he learned from church. Jaden was part of the church choir, singing from an open window outside. He loved visiting the church with Farmer Joe every Sunday. Today was Sunday, but he could not go because Farmer Joe was not there.

Every Sunday, Jaden was up early and ready. He waited outside Farmer Joe's door, and as soon as the farmer was ready to go, Jaden joined him trotting at his heels and followed him to the church. The church was just a little distance from Farmer Joe's farm. It was small and somewhat run-down, but Jaden loved it regardless. Some of his other siblings accompanied them to the church at times, but mostly it was just Farmer Joe and Jaden. Jaden was so regular at going to the church that he had made a lot of friends there. He also valued the visits to the church because it was Jaden and Farmer Joe's quality time together alone. On their way back, Farmer Joe often told Jaden stories about how his days were going, how his health had been, and what the neighbors were up to. He had been complaining of back pain for the past 3 weeks, but he kept putting off seeing a doctor.

Jaden wondered if his friends at church would miss him that day. "Guess I'll find out next week."

Jaden worked for another 2 hours, and by the time he was done, the field was clear. All the shrubbery and cut-off grass was piled up in a huge stack at the corner of the field.

The field was almost unrecognizable. For a year, they could not see the ground there, and now there it was—dry and caked.

"By the time I'm done with this, this will be a pretty field with lots of vegetables." As he admired his work, he realized just how tired he was. He put the hand pruner aside and called it a day. He would continue with the work tomorrow. Jaden wiped the sweat off his brow and sat down to rest for a bit. The cool breeze carried the sound of people laughing and running. He could distinctively make out Abe's voice among them.

"They've started playing without me!" he thought.

He quickly got up and raced off toward the field. He could see some of his siblings already starting to gather.

Chapter 7: Dawson

Meanwhile, Dawson and Landon had started work in the barn. Avery put the two of them together because she knew the barn was going to take a lot of time and effort. They had been assigned to clean out the barn and make it look presentable.

While Landon was chattering, carrying the supplies, Dawson was quiet as the huge barn came into view. There were hardly any animals left in Farmer Joe's barn. At one time, when the fainting goats were little, the farm was full of lots of animals—cows, horses, pigs, hens, sheep, and even a duck. As a young goat on the farm, Dawson was intrigued by all of them. He quickly became friends with most of them, and some of his fondest memories were when all the animals used to play together and chase each other around the farm. Farmer Joe would get frustrated and would then try to separate them to keep them from making any more noise.

As Farmer Joe got older and all the burden of responsibility fell on him, he could not keep up. Gradually, he started giving his animals away to friends who were interested in buying them, in the hope that they will be better taken care of at other farms. Eventually, all that was left on the once-busy farm were the fainting goats.

Under no condition was Farmer Joe willing to part with his beloved fainting goats. He had seen to them since they were brought to the farm, and with every passing day, he had grown even more attached to the goats. He could not bear to say goodbye to his goats. So, while all the other animals left, the fainting goats stayed.

Dawson always had a hard time saying goodbye. The animals had lived and grown up together on the farm, and Dawson considered them as much a part of his family as the goats. Every time someone was leaving the farm, Dawson would get sad and mope around all day. While all the goats would get sad, Dawson took everything to heart. Even when his siblings tried to cheer him up, it would not work. Some of his older brothers would make fun of him sometimes for being so emotional, but Farmer Joe would always take Dawson aside and tell him that his sensitivity was a gift, and his ability to feel things on a deeper level than the rest was his strength. He urged him never to lose it, and never to view it as a weakness. Dawson used to feel better after Farmer Joe's pep talks.

Standing at the entrance of the barn, Dawson thought back to how this same barn would always be filled with the animals and how noisy and messy it used to be. Dawson himself used to hang out there a lot. Dawson felt tears prickling his eyes; he missed his friends terribly.

He shook his head and wiped his eyes with the back of his hoof.

"No, I can't do this right now. I need to get things in order for Farmer Joe," he thought to himself.

Landon saw Dawson wiping away his tears and started snickering.

"Aww, Dawson misses his friends," he said in a teasing way, wiping away fake tears from his own eyes.

Dawson gave his little brother a light push and ordered him to start working.

Dawson looked around at the messy barn and made a list of the things that needed to be done. There was a lot of work; the barn was in a terrible condition. Haystacks were rotting away in the corner of the barn, and the floor was muddy. There was a broken tap on the side, which kept leaking water all over the floor, making everything soggy and disgusting. The light bulb at the top was not working anymore and the walls needed a good coat of paint.

"One thing at a time, Dawson," he said out loud to himself. "Landon, you start fixing the water tap, as Avery told you to, while I carry out the haystacks. When you are done, we can start cleaning up the floor together."

"Sure, boss," said Landon, and made a hard salute, stomping his hoof on the ground.

Bit by bit, Dawson carried the rotting haystacks outside and piled them up. Since his little hooves could carry only some at a time, even this simple task took him a while. He started adding numbers in his head to keep himself from getting bored: $10 \times 10 = 100$, $15 + 25 = 40$, $75 - 30 = 45$. Dawson loved numbers, and in an hour the barn was clear of all the rotting haystacks. He then moved out random tools and materials that Farmer Joe had left stacked in the corners. When he was done, the barn was clear of everything, and the floor and walls were bare and visible.

Landon was still busy working at his tap, grunting and grumbling.

"Hey, do you need any help with that?" Dawson called out.

"How about you do the entire thing for me," Landon replied, with big puppy

Landon
Dawson

dog eyes.

Dawson rolled his eyes; he was not going to fall for it.

"No, finish your work. I'm waiting."

Ten minutes later, Landon announced that he was done, but Dawson was still lost in thought about his old friends at the barn and did not hear him.

Suddenly, Dawson was hit by a strong jet of water, smack in the face. As he opened his eyes, squirting out water from his mouth, he saw Landon holding a hose in his hand and laughing uncontrollably.

"I thought I'd demonstrate to you that I have fixed the water tap!" gasped Landon, while cackling with laughter.

Dawson angrily darted toward him. Landon started running away, but slipped and fell in the puddle at his feet.

Now it was Dawson's turn to laugh as a red-faced, embarrassed Landon stood up. Both faced each other, dripping wet and within a minute both were laughing at themselves and at each other.

The tap was fully functional now. Landon turned it on and off and started dancing along the clean barn floor, celebrating.

"There is still a lot of work left, you know," Dawson remarked.

"Party pooper," Landon whispered underneath his breath.

Next they turned on the repaired tap and let the water flow until it covered the entire barn floor. Treading carefully, Dawson took a scrub brush and started scrubbing the floor and instructed Landon to do the same. There were layers of mud and straw caked on the floor of the barn, and Dawson was exerting himself hard to clean the floor. The goats used to play hide-n-seek in the barn because the dark, stuffy barn had plenty of places where they could successfully hide from one another.

Dawson and Landon worked away at the grimy floor, scrubbing and scrubbing. Occasionally, Dawson would correct what Landon was doing, and at times they were tossing soapy foam at each other. It was hard work, but Dawson was willing to put in the effort for the delightful smile on Farmer Joe's face when he sees what a good job the fainting goats had done. Though tiring, they were both having fun. When you work together, even the hardest of work does not seem so difficult or boring anymore. Dawson got down on his knees and scrubbed some more. He was sweating from the exertion, but he was so focused on his work that he lost track of time while working. After enough scrubbing, they got a big hose, which they had trouble lifting, and turned on the water. The gushing water took all the mud away, revealing a squeaky clean, gray concrete floor. They looked at each other delightedly and then turned the hose upward and let the water rain down on them as they danced around the barn happily.

Though Dawson was beaming at how clean he had managed to make the barn look, he could feel his muscles aching now. He was tired. Very tired. He figured they deserved a break.

"The only thing that's left to do now is to paint the walls. We can easily finish it by tomorrow," he reassured himself and his brother.

It was 4 o'clock when he checked the time. Avery had asked them to meet her in the same spot at 5 o'clock. Dawson sat under a tree and started counting numbers in his head while relaxing in the cool shade of the tree. Landon ran off toward the field.

"Where are you going?" Dawson called out, but Landon was already out of earshot.

"Probably off to make trouble somewhere," Dawson figured. He was too tired to think about it further and continued counting: $2 + 2 = 4$, $4 + 4 = 8$, $8 + 8 = 16$, $16 + 16 = 32$, $32 + 32 = 64$, and so on. He was soon snoring.

Chapter 8: Landon

Landon took out his packet of chewing gum and popped one into his mouth. He always took care not to let his siblings see his packet of gum, because then they would each want a piece. Landon saved his pocket money to get his pack every week, and though he knew that sharing is caring, he always made an exception to the rule for his gum.

Landon kept thinking about the fun Dawson and he had with the hose—how a minute ago Dawson was so sad and serious, and then the next moment they were both standing there dripping wet. "Well, at least I managed to cheer Dawson up," thought Landon. He knew the sight of the farm was making Dawson sad; they all knew Dawson was sensitive that way. They cared deeply about him and tried to cheer him up as best as they could.

Working in the barn was not even half as boring as Landon had anticipated. After some time, he went back to the barn to find out what Dawson was doing. Poor Dawson was once again working busily near the door of the barn. He was mending the broken wooden door that was hanging dangerously on its bottom last hinges. Landon started cleaning the wooden crates at the back of the barn, where he found a pair of Farmer Joe's old rubber boots. He looked at Dawson. Another mischievous idea occurred to him.

Landon looked at the boots and grinned to himself. Dawson was so occupied with work that there was no way Landon's sneaky little idea could fail this time. Quietly, he slipped on Farmer Joe's rubber boots. He took one deep breath, heaved his chest, pulled back his shoulders, and tried to mimic Farmer Joe's walk. One long stride at a time. When he was just 2 feet away from Dawson, who was still hammering loudly on the hinges, nailing the door to the door frame, Landon imitated Farmer Joe's voice and said out loud gruffly, "What do you think you are doing, Dawson?"

Dawson jumped up in surprise, lost his balance, and fell headfirst on the ground. Landon was rolling on the floor with laughter. In between the laughter and heavy breathing, he managed to say, "I got you so BAD!" Poor Dawson's white furry face was matted with dust and loose hay. He wiped off his face, collected his tools, and muttered, "It's not funny, Landon. I could have gotten hurt."

Landon tried to gain his composure. He rose to his feet, still wearing Farmer Joe's old rubber boots and said, "Okay, okay. I am sorry, Dawson. I should not have done that. But gosh, how you fell!" With that said, he once again broke into hysterical laughter and started clapping his hoofs together with glee.

But this time, the joke was on Landon. Dawson watched in amusement as Landon was inching closer and closer to the pail of water behind him. Dawson had filled this pail of water to scrub the barn door clean after he was done fixing it. Landon was laughing hysterically, clapping loudly and slowly moving backward just when his rear left leg collided with the pail, and Landon stumbled backward. The pail of water went up in the air and came crashing down, splashing all the water on Landon's face and chest.

Dawson was looking at all this play out with a dazed smile. But his smile quickly turned into concern as he saw Landon curl up in pain. Landon was still lying flat on his back. His face was red with embarrassment, and his eyes were swelling up with tears of pain. Dawson rushed toward Landon and asked him what had happened. Landon pointed at his knee and just muttered, "It hurts!" Dawson checked Landon's knee for signs of an injury, but there were no cuts or bruises. He touched Landon's knee, and Landon wailed in pain. "Ouch! It hurts!" Dawson knew Landon was exaggerating, but as his older brother, he still wanted to make sure that Landon was not hurt badly.

Dawson wiped off the water from the barn floor using a ragged piece of cloth. Farmer Joe always used to tell them to stay clear of wet floors while he would be mopping them. He had taught them that wet floors were slippery and could result in serious injuries. As Landon's older and responsible big brother, Dawson quickly wiped the floor dry, picked up the empty pail, and put it out of the way.

Next, he removed the rubber boots and placed them back in the wooden crate. He knew that if Landon tried to get up while still wearing Farmer Joe's big rubber boots, he would trip again. He went back to help Landon get back up on his feet. Landon was still moaning in pain. Dawson knew he was being a drama queen. Landon loved it when Dawson would become the older, loving, and more responsible brother. In fact, they all loved it when Dawson would care for them. Dawson didn't mind. He was the peacemaker and the soft-hearted goat in the family.

Dawson extended his right hand toward Landon and said, "Come on! Hold my hand and get up! We have a lot of work to do." Landon took Dawson's hand, but instead of getting up, he pulled Dawson down and rolled on top of him, ruffling his hair and tickling him in the belly. Dawson shrieked and giggled, all at the same time, "Stop, Landon! Oh gosh! Stop! Get off me!" But Landon continued to tease and tickle his older brother.

When he was finally done, and they both got up, Dawson playfully punched him in the chest and said, "I knew that you weren't hurt. You were just pretending the whole time. Now stop fooling around. We really have to finish all the work before Farmer Joe comes home." Landon straightened himself up and said, "Right! Right! I will clear the boxes from the back, and you get back to fixing the door."

But when has the fun ever stopped when Landon is in the house? Being the second most playful goat in the family after Miles, Landon's mischiefs were always a source of entertainment and a little bit of a worry for the others.

Just 3 days ago, Landon had played another naughty trick on the animals on another farm. He had bought this toy flower that looked just like a real flower but squirted water from its center when you pushed the button at the back.

First, he went to Miss Henny Penny and asked her to smell his lovely pink flower. As soon as she leaned in to smell the flower, Landon pressed the button at the back, and Miss Henny Penny flinched in shock as she was splashed with water. Soaking wet and fuming with anger, she chased Landon across the barn but gave up when her tiny feet couldn't match the pace of Landon's long legs.

Next, he decided to play this trick on Anne, the youngest daughter of Mrs. Quack. Anne was a young duckling and hardly ventured alone in the barn. But that day seeing her alone under the maple tree gave Landon the perfect opportunity to play his prank on her. He showed Anne his flower and asked her to sniff it. Poor Anne! As she curiously leaned in to sniff the pretty pink flower, she too was splashed with water. She ran back toward the pond, scared, drenching wet, and confused.

Just as Landon was thinking who he should fool next, Avery appeared from behind the tree and took the toy flower from his hand. As Landon tried to take back the flower with protest, Avery scolded him for disturbing Miss Henny Penny and Anne and said she would keep the flower with her until he went to them and apologized. She went to Farmer Joe and gave the flower to him for safekeeping.

Realizing his mistake, later in the day, Landon personally went to Miss Henny Penny and Anne to apologize for his naughty behavior, and this time, he took real pink flowers for both of them. They happily forgave him and accepted the pretty flowers.

But at night, when Farmer Joe had returned his toy flower to him, Landon continued to squirt water on Miles and his other goat brothers for fun.

Even while working in the barn, Landon and Dawson were constantly fooling around and cracking up at silly jokes. Landon was having so much fun that he forgot to feel tired.

Landon was so charged up that he could have continued working, but they realized that there was only a little time left until they were required to report to Avery.

Jaden
Landon
BOOo

While on their way over to the field, Landon saw Jaden running off in the same direction. As mischievous as ever, he just couldn't let an opportunity go by. He was sure Jaden had not seen him, so he quickly hid behind a tree. Jaden was coming toward him in full speed—all that training with Abe had really served him well. But as Jaden got closer to Landon, Landon jumped out suddenly and stood in his way and shouted, "BOO!"

Jaden shrieked in shock and tried to brake with his feet, but he could not because of the speed he was running at. He crashed into Landon, and both went tumbling and rolling down the hill. Landon was laughing while Jaden was screaming, "What is wrong with you, Landon?"

After a few minutes of freely tumbling down the hill, they came to a halt. Both were rubbing their heads and feeling dizzy. Landon tried opening his eyes, but it seemed the world was spinning. As things got better and Landon came to his senses, he opened his eyes to see Avery peering down at him.

"Uh-oh!" he thought.

Chapter 9: Miles

Miles was happy that Avery had assigned him with the task of painting the fence. He had thought it was easy work and it was more interesting than cleaning out the barn or planting the field. Even so, an hour into the work, he had started to get bored.

He tried to stifle multiple yawns and gave himself cheerful pep talks about how happy Farmer Joe was going to be when he saw his favorite fence freshly painted in red. He pictured Farmer Joe patting his head and telling him that Miles had done the best job out of everyone. Despite all his self-motivation, he could resist no more, and when Easton and Abe were out of sight, it was then that he had made his way to a nearby tree and settled down for a quick nap. He had set the paint can down beside him and promised himself that he would rest his eyes only for a few minutes.

But poor Miles fell into a deep sleep. When he was shaken awake to find Easton and Abe looking down at him, he was scared that they would be angry. But they seemed to be amused and could not stop smiling. Miles was so thankful that they were not mad at him for lazing around. He didn't think much of it and rushed back to his work.

This time, Miles tried to paint the fences with his full attention. With his tongue rolling out of his mouth in focus, he carefully ran his brush up and down the wooden fence, just like Easton had taught him. Out of the corner of his eye, he could see both his brothers eyeing him amusedly from time to time.

"They are probably keeping an eye on me to see if I fall asleep again," Miles figured.

Miles

But then he started noticing that even the animals that were passing by from their farms were also giggling and chuckling looking at him. He ignored it the first few times, thinking they must be laughing at something else. But after a while, it was clear that it was HIM they were laughing at.

"Oh, man!" Miles exclaimed loudly when he happened to look down at himself. His perfectly white fur was stained red from the paint. How did this happen? He was confused. He had been careful not to get too close to the paint.

But he could not help but laugh at himself too. The thought that he must look comical to others cracked him up.

He shrugged. Nothing could be done about it, so he might as well get on with his work. For the rest of the day, he worked hard on the fence, while the occasional cackle of laughter behind him continued. Every time he saw someone pointing at him and laughing, he puffed out his chest and made funny faces back at them. Miles never missed an opportunity to laugh.

The sun had almost made its way across the sky when Miles was done with his work for the day. Half of the fence line was still not repaired and thus could not be painted yet. Easton said that they will finish the work the next day and that this was enough for one day. Miles was relieved. He could hear his brothers in the field by now, and he could not wait to join them.

"Hey, Easton. Is there anything else I can do for you today?" he asked while sitting with Abe by the fence.

"Nope, you can go play," Easton stated.

"Yay!" Miles dropped his can of paint and ran over to where he could hear Landon and Jaden in the field. As he drew nearer, he could see Avery there too, and Jayce sprawled at her feet.

Giggling loudly, he approached the group, but as soon as everyone saw his face, they stopped what they were doing and stared at Miles instead, with their mouths gaping open.

"I know, I know. Don't I look red hot?" said Miles while twirling around and trying to model.

All of them burst out laughing. Even Avery. They were gasping for breath, and something told Miles that he was not in on the joke.

"Dude, your face!" Landon managed to gasp in between his laughter.

Miles' smile slipped off his face for a minute.

"My face?" His hoof reached up to touch his face ... and came away RED!

"Wait, what?" He ran to the edge of the field where there was a small pond and peered into the water. A face peered back at him with a red nose and red-stained cheeks. He looked absurd!

The others were still laughing behind him. Miles put his face in the water and tried to scrub the paint away. Although he managed to get the paint out, his face was still red with the embarrassment as he walked back to his siblings.

Easton and Abe had also made their way over by now and were telling the rest of them how they painted his face while he was sleeping under the tree.

As everybody continued laughing, Miles started joining in too. It was funny when he thought about it, and within minutes, all of them were rolling around on the ground, with their legs up in the air, laughing uncontrollably.

Chapter 10: Jayce

"**W**here has Farmer Joe gone?" asked Jayce in his regular high-pitched voice.
"To the hospital," replied Avery, without looking at him.

"Why? Is he going to die?" asked Jayce with his eyes wide open.

"Of course not," replied Avery, with a scowl on her face. "He's coming back in a day or two."

"Oh, he's going to be so happy when he sees his farm!" exclaimed Jayce, excitedly rubbing his hooves together.

Avery nodded without answering. Jayce had been talking nonstop since he started walking with Avery toward the barn.

"Will I get to paint too?" asked Jayce.

"We will see," replied Avery.

Avery had taken up the task of painting the outside walls of the barn. She was passionate about painting anyway and was a gifted artist, so who better for the job than her? She was contemplating painting a mural of Farmer Joe on the wall, though it might prove to be too difficult.

She had taken Jayce with her as she could definitely use some help. But part of the reason she had chosen Jayce to come along was that she knew that she is the only one who he would listen to. She knew she would have to put

Avery
Jayce
59

up with constant questions all day, but she adored Jayce, so she signed him up to help her.

Jayce then launched into a story about how he had painted a flower on Farmer Joe's front steps, and how much Farmer Joe loved it.

"Yeah, yeah, I'm sure you have great artistic skills. That is why I asked you to help me," said Avery.

Avery and Jayce first cleaned the wooden walls of the barn from the outside. They took a clean, damp rag and wiped down the walls. Then they used some polish to shine them up. It took some rubbing and scrubbing, but when they were both done, the barn walls looked as good as new.

"Oh, wow, we are done so early! I think we beat everybody!" said Jayce, jumping around.

"No, Jayce, we aren't done yet. We are going to paint a mural on top of this," explained Avery to the excited little goat.

"Mural? What is a mural?" inquired Jayce as his forehead puckered up.

"A mural is a painting done on a wall." Avery sighed as she started explaining to Jayce what a mural was and what she had in mind for Farmer Joe.

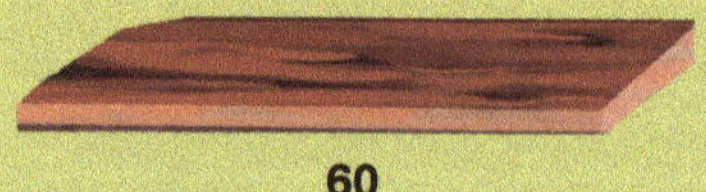

"Listen, how about we play a game?" suggested Avery to Jayce.

"What kind of game?" asked Jayce, perking up.

"For an hour, you cannot ask me any questions whatsoever. Just stay quiet and work. Can you do that?"

Jayce hesitated. "How long is an hour?" "How will I know when an hour is up?" He did not like the sound of this game, but then he agreed.

Avery sighed with relief. Jayce had been asking her questions since they started. And even before she could finish one answer, Jayce had a new question ready for her.

Avery needed him to stop talking so she could concentrate on the mural she was planning to paint. She had a great idea in mind but was uncertain if it would turn out well.

She wanted to paint a mural of Farmer Joe's face, surrounded by all eight of his beloved fainting goats. She assumed that it would make Farmer Joe happy—it could be his "family photo." The fainting goats were the closest thing to a family that Farmer Joe had for a very long time. Not even once had Avery seen any relatives or family members visiting Farmer Joe; he had always been on his own.

The goats and Farmer Joe had one picture together, in which the goats were babies. All of them were beaming up at the camera. The photo was taken at least 5 years ago, and you could see that Farmer Joe was in considerably better health back then. The photo was taken by Farmer Matt's son when he had come to visit from the city. He had a small, flashy camera in hand that he was constantly carrying and snapping pictures with. Once when Farmer Joe had been out in his field playing with the fainting goats, he had clicked a picture of them together, and to this day, it remains their only picture together. The picture still hung in Farmer Joe's bedroom, in a plain black frame, collecting dust.

"This could be our second family picture," Avery thought to herself. Her mural could be a gift to Farmer Joe, in which she would try to show how they all look currently. Something told her that there was nothing else Farmer Joe could love more than this.

She glanced at Jayce, who was working quietly on fixing all the places that had chipped marks.

Avery picked up a pencil and started drawing an outline that she could paint.

For half an hour, Avery worked with full concentration. She was focused on getting her outline right. Drawing Farmer Joe proved to be easier than she had thought, but she was really struggling with the goats. She had drawn Jayce, Landon, and Miles, and was working on Dawson when the air was pierced by an excited shriek.

"IS THAT ME?" screamed Jayce as he ran over to take a closer look at Avery's drawing. He was pointing at Landon though.

"No, I'm not going to draw you."

"What? Why not?"

"Because you are not letting me concentrate."

"Oh, I'm sorry. I'll let you work in peace now. Please don't leave me out of the mural."

Avery laughed. Jayce actually looked upset, so she assured him that everybody was going to be in the mural.

"Can I help? I can draw myself," Jayce offered.

"Absolutely not!" replied Avery.

"But you can help me paint it when I'm finished drawing an outline," she added when she saw Jayce's sad face. "How about you take a break for now?"

She watched Jayce as he walked off toward the field. "I better be done with the outline before he returns so we can start painting," she thought.

Jayce slipped through a crack in the fence into Farmer Matt's farm where there were two little lambs that Jayce had gotten close to. The lambs welcomed him excitedly, and Jayce got lost in telling them all about the exciting things the goats were doing for Farmer Joe. The lambs oohed and aahed and asked almost as many questions as Jayce did.

When Jayce finally ran back to Avery, he saw her standing 10 feet away from the wall, staring at it with a big smile on her face.

"Jayce, come here. Look!" she invited him excitedly.

As Jayce came nearer, the drawing started taking form to him.

"WOW!" he exclaimed in awe, eyes wide open. "You are brilliant, Avery!"

Avery laughed and shrugged her shoulders, but inside, she was gloating over the mural.

"Yeah?" Does it look okay?"

"Okay? It looks AMAZING!" screamed Jayce. "Oh boy, I can't wait to show the others what we have done."

"Hold your horses, Jayce. Let's paint it and then reveal the final thing to the others by evening."

She handed him a paintbrush and taught him to trace the outline with black paint. Jayce, though young, was a fast learner and quickly picked up on the correct way to hold and use a paintbrush. It automatically put a halt to Jayce's questions for a while as they both worked together.

When the outline was darkened, it was time to fill in the mural with paint to make it come to life. Again, Avery taught Jayce how to use paints, and how to blend them to get the right color and texture.

"One day, I'm going to paint as good as you do, Avery," he stated.

They worked for another 2 hours, and by the time they were done, the wall was alive with a painting of Farmer Joe and his eight fainting goats.

Chapter 11: Success of Working Together

All the fainting goats were happily chattering among themselves, laughing at Miles' red face, playing and joking around with each other, and telling each other about what they had done throughout the day. Avery joined in for a while, before she called the group to order.

"Okay, guys, enough talk. I need updates on what has been done and what is left. Let's start with Easton, shall we?"

And so, one by one, each goat told her what they had done all day, and how long it would still take for them to finish up.

Jayce was bursting to brag about the mural that Avery and he had worked on, so as soon as it was his turn, he insisted that everyone come see the mural for themselves.

The other goats were curious and followed Jayce to the barn wall.

The goats all lined up in front of the mural. They stood there staring up at the larger-than-life portrait of themselves and Farmer Joe. Nobody said a word.

"So, how is it?" asked Avery nervously.

"It is … incredible!" exclaimed Abe first, and the others soon joined in, gushing over how brilliantly Avery and Jayce had painted it.

Avery then stomped her hooves to get everyone's attention. "Farmer Joe is returning tomorrow at 5 p.m. Will we all be done by then?"

Jaden
Avery
Easton
Abe
Landon
Milos
Jayce
Dawson
67

"Yes!" came a synchronized answer.

The goats ate the food Farmer Matt had prepared for them, played a bit, and then settled in to sleep.

"It's a big day tomorrow, guys. Get some sleep!" was the last thing they heard Avery say. They all quickly fell asleep, as they were very tired.

The next day, the goats were up early. After breakfast, each went off to finish the work they had started the previous day. Avery had given them a deadline of 3 p.m., and they were supposed to report back to her to make sure everything was in order to welcome back Farmer Joe.

Easton and Abe went off to finish work on the fence, with a sleepy Miles tagging along with his paint can and rubbing his eyes.

Jaden headed over to his field with a spade and various packets of seeds in his hands.

Dawson and Landon each picked up a can of paint and headed over to paint the inside walls of the barn.

Avery watched all of them go, with Jayce at her heels.

"We have nothing to do today, so you can go help out Miles paint the fence if you wish," she said to Jayce.

Jayce bounded off happily toward Miles, and both started painting the fence together, chattering consistently.

By 3 p.m., all the goats were back. The work on the farm was complete. Now all that was left was to get ready to welcome Farmer Joe. The goats could no longer wait.

Chapter 12: Welcome Back, Farmer Joe!

The eight fainting goats lined up along the edge of the farm looking clean and proper as they waited for Farmer Joe to show up. Avery had ordered all of them to take a dip in the pond and become presentable before Farmer Joe's arrival.

As they stood waiting impatiently, they saw Farmer Joe's truck appear on the far end of the road. The old truck made its way slowly along the dirt road and came to a sputtering halt right in front of them. Farmer Matt was driving, and he helped Farmer Joe out of his truck.

As soon as Farmer Joe saw his darling goats waiting for him, he limped toward them and gave each one a big hug.

He was beaming from ear to ear as he kissed each one of them on the head. The goats surrounded him as he greeted them all.

It was a moment before Farmer Joe registered that the farm looked different. With a bewildered expression, he first looked at the freshly painted red fence, and then at the planted field, and then at the shiny barn in the distance.

"What happened here?" he muttered to nobody in particular.

The goats said nothing but waited for him to realize it himself.

"Oh, my goodness, did you guys do this?" he exclaimed when he started to realize what had happened.

The eight fainting goats nodded in unison.

"Oh, my goodness!" he repeated. "I can't believe this!" He started walking toward the barn. His expression was an equal mixture of surprise and happiness, and he seemed like he was at a loss for words.

He passed by the freshly planted field, now ready to start growing vegetables, and the spotless, clean barn.

And then he noticed the mural. He stopped in his tracks. Avery saw tears spring to his eyes as he looked at the beautiful mural of him and his goats.

"Welcome back, Farmer Joe. We missed you. We hope this was a nice surprise for you," said Avery.

"I ... I don't know what to say, guys. You did this all for me?" he asked, his eyes still stuck on the mural.

Once again, the goats only nodded.

"I love it so much! I don't know how to thank you all for this. Everything looks beyond beautiful!" he exclaimed, a tear finally rolling down his cheek.

"You don't have to. You do so much for us every day. We just wanted you to know that you are very dear to us. Besides, we had so much fun working together to repair the farm. Right, guys?"

"Yes!" bleated all the goats.

"We love you, Farmer Joe," they said as they all closed in for a huge group hug. All of them were crying happy tears as Farmer Joe held each of them in his loving arms.

Farmer Joe broke away sooner than the goats wanted. He stepped back, wiping the tears away from his eyes. With his eyes lit up, he announced, "I have a little surprise for you guys too. Follow me."

"Yay, I love surprises!" exclaimed Miles, jumping ahead of the rest of them and racing up to keep up with Farmer Joe. Farmer Joe headed back to his truck. Farmer Matt was standing beside the truck, fussing with something in the backseat.

As he saw Farmer Joe approaching with his group of goats trailing behind him, he smiled and stepped aside.

Farmer Joe reached inside the truck, and with some huffing and puffing he pulled out a small bundle of white fur.

The eight fainting goats stood at the edge, standing on tiptoes to see what Farmer Joe was holding.

None of them were tall enough to see though. Miles and Jayce stepped closer. They were so curious that they forgot their constant stream of questions.

Farmer Joe kneeled on the grass so that the goats could have a better look. He just stared at them, waiting for them to get over their shock.

Jaden
Dawson
73

Boy, this was not what any of them were expecting when he said there was a surprise for them.

Bundled up in Farmer Joe's arm, with its eyes barely open, was a newborn fainting goat.

"Say hello to your new sibling!"

Chapter 13: An Unexpected Guest

"Who is this?" asked Avery cautiously.

"And why is it here?" added Miles stubbornly.

"This is … well, I have not decided on a name yet. Maybe you guys can help me with it," he suggested.

None of them said anything. They were too busy staring at the new baby goat. It was a tiny little thing. It had short, white fur, with just a speck of black on the head. Its eyes were more like black beads, and it was too small to understand what was happening.

"This baby goat is going to live with us now. It will be a little addition to our family," declared Farmer Joe.

Though none of them said anything, Farmer Joe knew them too well.
He let out a hearty laugh.

"I love you all, and this baby goat does not mean my love for you will be any less. You can never be replaced," he reassured them.

"You promise?" asked Landon in a small voice.

"Of course! Come here, all of you."

With Farmer Joe's reassurance, the goats felt better and swarmed around him. He set the baby goat down on the grass, but its legs were too weak, and it stumbled and fell on the grass.

76

All the eight goats found it hilarious and adorable. They laughed and put out curious hooves to touch the baby. Within minutes, the goats were so involved with the little one that they forgot all about Farmer Joe.

Over the next few days, the farm was a flurry of activities as all the eight goats revolved around the baby goat. All of them wanted to be near it, to touch it, to sleep with it, to teach it how to walk. Farmer Joe had to constantly remind them to give the baby goat some space, as it was still very young.

The goats made a soft, comfortable bed for the baby goat in the barn. As soon as the baby would wake up, they would want it to come play with them. Farmer Joe again had to intervene and explain that it was too small to play with them just yet.

"I can't wait for it to grow older and join us," said Jaden one day, his eyes filled with love.

It was heartwarming watching the eight goats adopt the addition so wholeheartedly. Farmer Joe could not help but beam with pride when he would see the goats fussing over the baby. He could tell they loved the baby goat, and he was so proud of them for how they had all stepped up in taking care of it. He could not have done all of it on his own if he didn't have the support of his eight beloved goats.

Oh, nine beloved goats, he reminded himself, smacking his own forehead.

Farmer Joe knew that even if in the coming months his health would start to fail him, the eight older fainting goats would find a way to cooperate and help one another in taking care of their youngest sibling, just like they had worked together to fix the farm in his absence.

But one thought made him chuckle. "We still haven't decided on a name for the little one." He decided to consult the eight fainting goats. After all, the baby goat was their younger brother, so the older siblings must have a say.

Farmer Joe went into the barn and was delighted to find them all there, huddled around the youngest one, who was tightly wrapped in a fluffy blanket.

Avery was standing nearest to him. She had a bottle of warm milk. She gently shook the bottle to mix the sugar well. As she turned the bottle over to let out a drop of milk on her hooves, Abe shrieked and snatched the bottle from her.

"Hey! You are dripping all his milk!" Abe said.

"I am not dripping his milk. I am tasting it to make sure it's sweet enough for him. He will not drink it if it is not sweet," replied Avery as she took back the bottle from Abe.

The others laughed as Abe's face turned red with embarrassment. Farmer Joe was watching all this play out from the entrance of the barn. The eight fainting goats never failed to amuse him. With a broad smile on his face, he wondered what mischief the youngest one would be up to once he was old enough to play and run around the farm with his older siblings.

As Avery continued to nurse the young one and the rest sat around them, huddled together in a circle, munching on their sweet, green grass, Farmer Joe entered the barn.

"Good morning, my darlings!" said Farmer Joe in his usual cheerful voice. "How is everyone doing today?" he inquired.

As soon as the goats heard his voice, they got up and ran to him. All except Avery. She smiled to him in acknowledgment, her hooves still carefully holding the milk bottle as the young one sucked on it.

Farmer Joe patted and cuddled all the seven goats one by one. He loved ruffling up their soft fur, especially Dawson's, who always took his appearance very seriously.

Farmer Joe let out a hearty laugh as Dawson quickly straightened his matted fur with his hooves. Others pushed past him, trotting behind Farmer Joe as he took his place beside Avery and the little one.

"Guys," said Farmer Joe, "today, I want your help with something very important." He paused to make sure everyone had heard him. And everyone had. They were all looking at him curiously, waiting for him to continue.

"We would love to help you, Farmer Joe. You can count on us for that," said Avery as she looked at the others for some moral support.

"Yeah! We do, Farmer Joe," they all said in unison.

"I knew I could count on you guys because this matter is of serious concern.

And I have been thinking about it for a long time, but I just can't seem to make up my mind," said Farmer Joe.

Easton looked troubled. He wondered if Farmer Joe was thinking about bringing another baby goat to the family, or worse—maybe he was thinking about sending them all away. His health had been failing him lately, and he would often tell them to keep the noise level down.

He gathered the courage to ask in his meek voice, "Farmer Joe, are you thinking about sending us away? Is it because we make too much noise?"

Farmer Joe laughed and said, "No, my darling! I would never send you away. I need you. This farm needs you. But most importantly, this new baby goat needs a NAME! This is why I want your advice, because I cannot do it alone. You are his older siblings. You would surely know what's best for him, right?"

He looked around for a response.

By now, they all had a big grin on their faces. They not only felt relieved to hear that they were not being sent away, but they also felt immensely important for being asked their advice. They nodded their heads excitedly.

"You are right, Farmer Joe," exclaimed Jayce.

Farmer Joe pushed them further, "So, what would you all like to name him?"
"Toothless!" came an immediate response from Landon.

"Landon!" Avery elbowed him in his chest. As the others laughed, Landon recoiled in pain.

Dawson bleated, "How about Cutie Pie? He is the cutest thing in the whole world!"

Abe frowned, "What kind of a name is Cutie Pie? Everyone on the farm will laugh at him. Farmer Joe, let's name him after a famous soccer player! I will coach him, and he will become famous!"

"No way!" responded Easton. "I want my brother to have a unique name. His name should be different."

"And special," Jayce completed the sentence excitedly.

"Then what should we name him?" Farmer Joe asked yet again as he looked around the room for responses.

They were lost deep in thought. Thinking of a name for their younger brother that would be just as unique and special as him.

Just then, the baby goat yawned loudly, and with his eyes still tightly shut, he let out a soft bleat "Mahhhhvvvvv," and snuggled back into his fluffy blanket. "Oh, my gosh! I think he just said his name," exclaimed Avery.

Everyone looked at her, utterly confused, including Farmer Joe.

"What do you mean, Avery?" Jaden asked.

Avery smiled and facepalmed her forehead. "You guys! He said Mav! It's short for Maverick!"

"I think it sounded more like Mac, you know, for mac and cheese," bleated Jayce.

"My darlings, let's just pay attention to what Avery has just said," stated Farmer Joe.

"M-A-V-E-R-I-C-K," said Farmer Joe. He slowly and clearly spelled out the name and was lost in deep thought. Suddenly, the deep furrows on his forehead became smooth, and his lips curled into a pleasant smile. He stood up and declared, "I love it! I absolutely love it. Good job, Avery!" He turned to the others and asked, "Guys, what do you think? Isn't Maverick a unique and special name?"

They all agreed!

"Then Maverick it is! From now on, you will call Maverick by his name. Soon the whole farm will follow suit. And as he grows older, he will learn to respond to his name, so if God forbid, he gets lost out in the field, he will come to us running when he hears his name being called out," said Farmer Joe.

"We will never let him graze the fields alone, Farmer Joe! We will always take good care of him and make sure that he never gets lost," said Dawson reassuringly.

"Yes, Farmer Joe," the others agreed.

"I know you all are very caring and responsible older siblings. I am really proud of you all," said Farmer Joe as he gave them all a group hug.

He picked up Maverick in his arms and took him inside the house for a warm bath.

Chapter 14: The Soccer Match

To celebrate Farmer Joe's return to health, the arrival of Maverick, and the newly repaired farm, Farmer Joe decided to invite some close friends and neighbors over for a small get-together. When he shared the idea with the fainting goats, they were extremely excited and had a few ideas of their own. "How about we organize a soccer match for the day?" exclaimed Abe.

"Is that all you think about?" asked Easton teasingly, but all of them were equally excited about it.

"I think it's a great idea," added Jaden. "Farmer Joe and his friends can sit on the side and watch."

"Yeah, and we can have lots of mac and cheese!" Jayce piped in.

Everybody laughed. Jayce could eat mac and cheese all day, every day.

"I'll make you some right now, Jayce. Do you want to help me?" asked Farmer Joe, stroking his head affectionately.

"You guys discuss what you want to do, and I'll make dinner," said Farmer Joe as he walked back inside the house with Jayce at his feet.

"We can have special t-shirts designed for our team to wear. We can also give some to the guests to wear as supporters. I can design the t-shirts and hand-paint them," said Avery, wanting to utilize her artistic skills.

"Oh boy, this is starting to sound better and better with every passing second!" exclaimed Easton. "Let's do this!"

"We'll all have to work together really hard to pull this off," warned Avery.

"That's not a problem. I think we make a great team," said little Miles, serious for once.

All the fainting goats looked at each other and smiled. After the farm repair, they could not agree more with Miles' statement.

They saw Farmer Joe waving to them from the farmhouse, calling them for dinner. The smell of delicious mac and cheese was gusting throughout the field, and they all ran inside. They have not had Farmer Joe's food in so long! At the dinner table, they had a cheerful meal, with all of them talking over each other. Maverick had a special chair on which he sat. He loved to look at his older siblings from his raised chair and bang at the detachable table with his spoon to draw attention. When he would have their attention, he would just giggle and gurgle.

But today, they were not letting him interrupt their important meeting.

They continued to discuss the plan for the day, and Farmer Joe gave them the go-ahead. The fainting goats knew that they had to spend the next two days preparing for the soccer match and a house party.

Early the next morning, Avery set out to collect her fabric paints. Farmer Joe gave her a bunch of his old plain colored t-shirts, and after thinking for a while, she carefully painted a sample t-shirt and held it up for Farmer Joe.

He loved the design and cheered her on, encouraging her further. She kept painting, and by lunchtime, she was ready with all the t-shirts, one for each of them.

Her brothers admired the t-shirts too and patted her on the back for doing such a good job. Meanwhile, Abe had taken control of organizing the match. He had been going around the neighborhood, along with Jaden and Easton, inviting other goats and animals to join the match. By evening they had a long list of their friends who had signed up to play in the soccer match.

Farmer Joe left them to it and went over to meet his friend, Farmer Matt. He boasted about how the goats had repaired his farm in his absence, and he invited him over for the match too.

"Of course, I'll be there. Who doesn't love a good old soccer match?" he said, laughing heartily.

Farmer Joe invited a few other friends and neighbors too. When he came home, he called Dawson to ask him to add up how much it would cost them to organize everything.

Dawson loved math, and he immediately sat down with a notepad and pencil to work on the calculations for the party. Together, they added the cost of the snacks, t-shirts, and decorations and arrived at a final amount. All the while, Farmer Joe was admiring how quick Dawson was with all the math. Farmer Joe handed Dawson the money and asked him to run to the market and buy the necessary materials.

In the evening, all the fainting goats and their friends gathered for a practice match. After a fun playoff for an hour, Abe called it a day.

"Everybody, go home and get a good night's sleep so you can perform well in the match tomorrow!"

Finally, it was the day of the soccer match. People had started gathering at the house. Farmer Joe was laughing and talking to his friends, who had formed a circle around him and were asking about his health and admiring Maverick, cooing over him.

The fainting goats and their friends were out in the fields. The match was supposed to start at 5 p.m. Soon, people started gathering by the side of the field. The two teams stood facing each other.

As Abe was delivering a pep talk to his team, he realized that his siblings were nervous about people watching.

"Listen, there's no need to be nervous. Just play and have fun. That's what we are here for."

Easton, Miles, and Jayce nodded. Even Landon seemed a little quieter than normal.

With a blow of the whistle from Farmer Joe, the match started. Abe and Jaden were shouting instructions to their siblings from the other end of the field.

Avery
Landon
Abe
Mile
Dawson

The soccer ball was in Miles' possession.

Farmer Joe was happily cheering them on. "Come on, Miles, you can do it!"

As soon as Miles looked up to locate Farmer Joe in the crowd, he saw a bunch of people staring back at him. And before he realized what was happening, he fainted. His legs were stiff, and all he could see was the blue sky above him. The crowd burst out laughing at the sight. Nobody was making fun of him, but the image of Miles on the ground in the middle of the bustling soccer field was an entertaining sight.

Cameron, the chubby piglet from the next farm, quickly grabbed the soccer ball from Miles, but he was laughing so hard that he quickly lost it to Avery. Cameron dropped to his knees from laughing and saw that Jayce had also fainted in the middle of the field. By then, Avery had passed the ball back to Miles.

Farmer Joe had figured out what was happening and was trying his best to make his goats relax. He was cheering them on loudly, so much so that Miles and the others could distinctively hear him above the noise of the rest of the crowd. Miles locked eyes with him directly and saw Farmer Joe's kind and concerned eyes and his encouraging smile. He was trying to make his beloved goats focus on him so they could feel at ease and continue playing. Miles got lost looking at Farmer Joe in adoration. The noises around him fell away, and all he could hear was Farmer Joe. He focused harder to make out what he was saying.

"Behind you, Miles!"

Miles quickly got back to his senses. Farmer Matt's shepherd dog, Thomas, had run up behind him and was trying to claim the ball for himself. Miles tried to distract Thomas.

"Knock, knock!" yelled Miles.

"Who's there?" Thomas barked.

"Ketchup!" bleated Miles.

"Ketchup who?" asked Thomas.

"Ketchup with me and I'll tell you!" yelled Miles as he swiftly ran ahead with the ball. His eyes were set on the goalpost in front of him, which was being guarded by a calf from a neighboring farm.

Thomas was closing in on him, and Miles knew he had to aim and shoot the ball right away. Thomas was bigger and stronger than him. Miles knew that if Thomas caught up to him, he could easily wrestle the ball away. Miles glanced one last time at Farmer Joe and kicked hard with all his might. He then shut his eyes tight.

The crowd erupted in a loud cheer!

Miles slowly opened his eyes to see if he had made it. He saw his team members running up to him to hug him. He saw the scorecard in Farmer Joe's hands as he raised it above his head, overjoyed with Miles' performance.

1-0, it read.

Miles finally allowed himself to laugh out loud. He could not believe it. He had scored the first goal!

Miles looked at Abe who looked the happiest of them all. Abe lifted Miles from the ground and was patting his back excitedly.

"Hey, big brother, was that cool?" asked Miles affectionately.

Abe ruffled his hair playfully and said, "Cool? That was AWESOME, Miles! That was greater than awesome! Keep playing like this and we will win!"

The bell rang loudly, alerting the players to get ready for the game to start again. Feeling significantly more confident now, Miles took his position and gave a huge thumbs-up to Farmer Joe.

The soccer ball rolled into Dawson's possession this time. He got so excited as soon as he had the ball that he, too, fainted. The crowd roared with laughter as Avery quickly took possession of the ball. She dodged everybody else, made it to the opposite goalpost, and scored!

As the other six goats ran up to Avery to hug her, Dawson looked sad, thinking it could have been him who was getting cheered like that. Farmer Joe was punching the air in excitement and happiness.

The card in his hand now read 2-0. Needless to say, by now, the opponents were panicking. The opposite team was being led by a horse named Wyatt.

Wyatt was tall and handsome, and from a farm owned by Mr. and Mrs. Duddley. He was a well-trained athlete and was known for his speed and stamina. He quickly motioned his team to huddle up and whispered instructions to them. Jayce, Easton, and Avery looked at Abe, but he told them to relax as they had the lead, and it was not easy for Wyatt's team to change the score.

The game continued. The fainting goats kept fainting from time to time, but within a few minutes they were focused on the game. The fainting eventually reduced as the goats got used to the attention and crowd.

But when Jaden fainted with the ball still in his possession, it worked in the favor of the other team. Cameron quickly kicked the ball away from Jaden and passed it on to Thomas. Thomas ran with the ball until he was just 10 feet away from the goalpost. In a swift motion, he kicked the ball to Cameron who wasted no time in hitting the ball right over Landon's head, who was the goalkeeper for Abe's team.

"Yes!" said Cameron excitedly as he walked past Abe and smirked, "Watch out, Abe! We are coming for you!"

The score was now 2-1. Abe told his team to stay calm and focused. They were still in the lead. The game continued and this time Abe took possession of the ball. He motioned Easton to cover him so that he could pass the ball to Dawson who was near the goalpost. But Emma and Nora, the twin ducks from the next-door farm, blocked Easton and so he wasn't unable to clear the path for Abe. Abe was ambushed by Thomas and Cameron, and even though he managed to kick the ball toward Avery, Cameron was too quick. He kicked the ball right out of Avery's reach and scored a goal.

Farmer Joe yelled from the stands, "No!" He tried to maintain his composure for the sake of his goats, but he was nervous. It was clearly visible from his clasped hands and the deep furrows on his forehead.

The scorecard now read 2-2.

Time was nearly up, and the crowd was counting down from 60 seconds. The situation in the soccer field was getting tenser by the second. Each team wanted to make another goal and win the game, but in their own excitement, they kept missing the chance and losing the ball to someone. Just as the countdown was down to 30, Easton quickly scooped in, stole the ball, and ran full speed toward the goalpost. Jaden, being a good runner too, ran after him to protect him from the opposing team and provide cover if need be. But even though Easton kicked the ball with his full might, the opposing team's goalkeeper stopped the ball and passed it right back to Cameron.

Both Cameron and Abe knew that these last few seconds were very crucial to the game. Whichever team would win this match, would be remembered for their glorious victory for years to come.

Jayce and Landon were breathing heavily. They were tired and were looking forward to yummy lunch that was waiting for them outside the soccer field.

The crowd chanted, "20, 19, 18, ..."

"What's the point now?" Jayce said to Landon, with a sad look in his eyes.

Just then, a figure dashed past them, screaming, "The game's not over guys!"

It was Dawson. He had the ball and was running toward the goalpost!

Landon and Jayce quickly got to their feet and ran after him. Just as Dawson approached the post, though, one of Farmer Matt's sheep, Riley, appeared out of nowhere, ready to take the ball away. Dawson realized he would not be able to save it. He quickly passed the ball on to Abe, who kicked it as hard as he could toward the goalpost.

"5, 4, 3, …."

The crowd erupted again! Abe could not believe it. He did it! He scored the goal!

He turned around as the crowd started flowing over to the soccer field. He saw Farmer Joe holding the scorecard up. It read 3-2! They had won the game! The eight fainting goats had won the soccer match!

He saw Farmer Joe running toward him with the scorecard still in his hands. Farmer Joe scooped him up in his arms, hugging him and laughing. The rest of the fainting goats also came running over and joined them, turning it into a big group hug, with all of them laughing, crying, and congratulating each other.

The moment was so full of joy and love. Farmer Joe's friends also patted the players on their heads and told them what a good game it had been. Cameron walked up to Abe and shook his hoof. "Good game, pal! Good game!" he said. "All of you go take a drink from the pond, clean up, and come to dinner." Farmer Joe called out to all of them before turning back and heading to the farm, with Maverick in his arms.

The eight fainting goats and their friends took a drink and a dip in the water. Pretty soon, it turned into a water fight, as they all splashed water on each other, squealing and screaming as they tried to avoid getting splashed on.

After a few minutes, Avery reminded them that they had to get back for dinner, so the group of friends made their way back.

"I'm starving!" said Riley, and ran ahead of the group.

"Race you to the food!" Jaden called out to Riley. They both ran, while the others slowly strolled along. Jaden won, of course. He was a great runner. The sheep was no match for Jaden.

At the house, they all filled their plates with all sorts of yummy snacks and food. Farmer Joe had made his famous chicken pie, and even mac and cheese on Jayce's request. With their tummies full, and their hearts content, the fainting goats and Farmer Joe spent the rest of the evening having a good time with friends.

Later, Avery, Abe, Easton, and Jaden helped Farmer Joe clean up after everybody else had gone home. They tucked Maverick in bed, and Avery sang a lullaby to get him to fall asleep as Jayce watched.

Farmer Joe got each of the fainting goats little presents and told them how proud he was of them for organizing such a fun-filled day. He thanked them for all the help and support they had given him in taking care of Maverick.

"You didn't get anything for Maverick," remarked Miles while opening his own present.

Farmer Joe laughed, "I think he's too young to recognize and appreciate gifts just yet."

"Don't worry, we'll share ours with him, so he doesn't feel left out," Dawson said, busy with his own present.

Farmer Joe's chest filled with pride and love at how kind and compassionate the eight fainting goats were becoming as they were getting older.

After showing off their gifts to each other, the eight little goats quit for the night as well, after giving Farmer Joe a goodnight hug and a kiss on the cheek.

They all fell asleep with big smiles on their faces and a warm feeling in their hearts, ready to greet the next day with the same excitement and hoping for a grand breakfast from Farmer Joe in the morning.

"It was my 9 Grandchildren that inspired me to write this Book. They are all very special and watching them grow is such a source of JOY! I was able to capture a bit of their individual personalities in this Story, which makes this Book even more heart warming. Thank you again, Grandpa Dale Bunkers, for portraying "Farmer Joe " in this Story. Your great grandchildren adore you and this makes the Story even more special.

At the time of this writing: Avery - 14 yrs, Abe - 11 yrs, Easton - 11 yrs, Jaden - 10 yrs, Dawson - 7 yrs, Landon - 7 yrs, Miles - 5 yrs, Jayce - 4 yrs, Maverick - 5 months

Special mention to the other great- grandchildren of Dale Bunkers in this story.
Wyatt - 1 yr; Cameron - 4 yrs; Riley - 2 yrs; Thomas - 6 yrs; Nora - 11 yrs; Emma - 13 yrs

www.ingramcontent.com/pod-product-compliance
Lightning Source LLC
Chambersburg PA
CBHW041151300726
48981CB00003B/219